STORIES OF
COOPERATION

CHERRY
LAKE
Publishing

Published in the United States of America by Cherry Lake Publishing
Ann Arbor, Michigan
www.cherrylakepublishing.com

Content Adviser: Satta Sarmah Hightower, www.sattasarmah.com
Reading Adviser: Marla Conn MS, Ed., Literacy specialist, Read-Ability, Inc.

Photo Credits: ©Joseph Sohm/Shutterstock Images, cover, 1; ©amanaimagesRF/Thinkstock Images, 5; ©Bob Orsillo/
Shutterstock Images, 7; ©William Orpen/Wikimedia, 8; ©NASA, 11; ©(NASA/Joel Kowsky), 13; ©Jeroen van den Broek/
Shutterstock Images, 15; ©vasara/Shutterstock Images, 16; ©reptiles4all/Shutterstock Images, 17; ©anusorn2005/Shutterstock
Images, 18; ©Ekkachai/Shutterstock Images, 21; ©Scott Prokop/Shutterstock Images, 22; ©Drop of Light/Shutterstock
Images, 25; ©Zephyr_p/Shutterstock Images, 27; ©Ron Zmiri/Shutterstock Images, 28

Library of Congress Cataloging-in-Publication Data
Names: Colby, Jennifer, 1971- author.
Title: Stories of cooperation / by Jennifer Colby.
Description: Ann Arbor : Cherry Lake Publishing, [2018] | Series: Social emotional library |
    Audience: Grade 4 to 6. | Includes bibliographical references and index.
Identifiers: LCCN 2017033502 | ISBN 9781534107434 (hardcover) | ISBN 9781534109414 (pdf) |
    ISBN 9781534108424 (pbk.) | ISBN 9781534120402 (hosted ebook)
Subjects: LCSH: Cooperation—Juvenile literature.
Classification: LCC HD2963 .C635 2018 | DDC 302/.14—dc23
LC record available at https://lccn.loc.gov/2017033502

Cherry Lake Publishing would like to acknowledge the work of The Partnership for 21st Century Learning.
Please visit www.p21.org for more information.

Printed in the United States of America
Corporate Graphics

ABOUT THE AUTHOR

Jennifer Colby is a school librarian in Michigan. She cooperates with teachers
to develop and teach lessons to her students.

TABLE OF CONTENTS

What Is Cooperation?

You like to try and get along with your friends and family, but it can be hard. Sometimes you need to talk with each other in order to work together to come to an agreement or solve a problem. Doing this is a great example of cooperation. Cooperation can happen between two people, between groups or countries, and even with animals. Many examples of cooperation can be found throughout history and around the world.

[21ST CENTURY SKILLS LIBRARY]

Games are more fun when you cooperate with others.

Treaty of Versailles

You know what war is. Countries have disagreements and decide that the only way to solve the problem is to fight with each other. But how do wars end?

Usually one country surrenders, but agreements must be made so that warring nations can trust one another. **Treaties** are created through cooperation in order to ensure long-lasting peace.

The Treaty of Versailles is one of the many treaties that brought World War I (1914-1918) to an end. It was signed between the **Allied forces** and Germany exactly five years after the **assassination** of Archduke Franz Ferdinand, which had sparked the series of events that started the war.

World War I was fought in Europe, Africa, Asia, and the Middle East between the **Central Powers** and the Allied forces.

WWI airplanes were used to watch and fight enemies.

It was referred to as a "world war" because up to 32 countries were involved at some point. The United States entered the war on April 6, 1917, because German submarines threatened French and British merchant ships. The war destroyed property, hurt relationships between countries, and took many lives.

In January 1918, the president of the United States, Woodrow Wilson, created a plan called the Fourteen Points. It suggested creating a League of Nations where the countries involved would cooperate in **diplomatic** ways. In the fall of 1918, the Central Powers collapsed and asked for a surrender based on the

William Orpen made a painting called *The Signing of Peace in the Hall of Mirrors.*

Fourteen Points. An **armistice** was signed on November 11, 1918, which ended fighting in Europe.

The Treaty of Versailles was signed on June 28, 1919. Although fighting had ended seven months earlier, it took a long time to **negotiate** a peace. Most of the treaty was agreed upon in 145 private meetings between the United Kingdom, France, the United States, and Italy. The remaining Allied countries gave their advice during weekly meetings. Germany was not part of the negotiations. The treaty forced Germany to give up its

[21ST CENTURY SKILLS LIBRARY]

weapons, give away territory, and, most importantly, take responsibility for "all loss and damages" during the war. The other countries felt that the stern **reparations** were necessary to keep Germany from gaining too much power again.

During the war Woodrow Wilson had said that to end it, "Only a peace between equals can last." There would have to be "a peace without victory." Though drafted through collaboration and cooperation among nations, the Treaty of Versailles did not bring a lasting peace. A mere 20 years later, Germany invaded Poland, and World War II began. All the nations of the world must cooperate to prevent war.

Are You Cooperative?

Do you get along with others? Do you work together to solve problems? If you do, then you are cooperative. Maybe you worked with others on a group project, or maybe you helped raise money for a good cause by organizing a car wash or a dance-a-thon. These are all examples of cooperation. Think about other ways that you are cooperative.

The International Space Station

Did you ever work on a school project with a group of students? Maybe you had to create a presentation or build a model. Can you imagine working with students from other countries—and creating that project in space? That is exactly what happened during the creation of the International Space Station (ISS). The ISS is a home in space for the world's astronauts and is about the size of a five-bedroom house. Built and maintained by the space **agencies** of the United States, Russia, Europe, Japan, and Canada, it is an excellent example of cooperation.

The main purpose of the ISS is to serve as a laboratory to perform experiments that cannot be done on Earth. The first crew to live on the ISS arrived on November 2, 2000. Ever since then, it has been continuously occupied. Finally completed

The ISS gets its power from solar energy.

in 2011, it took 13 years to build—the first piece of the station was delivered to space by a Russian rocket in 1998. Building the facility required an enormous amount of planning, communication, and cooperation. Throughout its construction, pieces of the space station were independently made by the **participating** space agencies. The pieces did not fit together until they were on location in space.

The ISS can support up to six crew members plus the occasional visitor. The space station is as long as a football field (including the end zones) and on Earth, it would weigh about 1 million

A Soyuz rocket launched on July 28th, 2017, to bring the Expedition 52 crew to the International Space Station.

pounds (453,592 kilograms). At any given time, crew members from any of the cooperating space agencies are living at the ISS. In the summer of 2017, a crew named Expedition 52 was living and working on the ISS. The crew included two Russian cosmonauts (the Russian term for astronauts), three American astronauts, and one Italian astronaut. Their mission was to investigate a new drug to fight bone loss, study the **physics** of **neutron stars**, and analyze the **adverse** effects of having no gravity weighing down the heart.

The space station is important because it provides an opportunity for humans to constantly be in space. Research done on the space station helps scientists learn more about medicine, agriculture, physical science, and space science. Everything they learn will help prepare humankind for space missions that go farther into space than ever before.

All the participating countries need to cooperate to operate the ISS. This effort involves international flight crews, launch vehicles (rockets), crew training, engineering, construction facilities, and research. The countries must continually work together to plan and maintain the ISS and all of its programs.

Daniel Green and His Seizure Snake

You have seen a service dog. It is trained to help its owner who may be blind or deaf or suffer from another disability. People and their service dogs work together to develop a cooperative relationship. The service dog helps the person navigate through daily life, while receiving love and care from its owner. But have you ever seen a service snake? Daniel Green has trained, and cares for, a snake that assists him every day.

Green has owned snakes before, but never one that could save his life. He has **epilepsy** and can experience multiple seizures per month. A seizure happens when a large electrical **surge** occurs in the brain, disrupting the normal flow of **neurons**. A person experiencing a seizure can exhibit limb twitching, muscle spasms, and a loss of **consciousness**. Seizures can cause permanent damage and even death.

14

Service animals do an important job and shouldn't be petted by strangers.

A red-tailed boa constrictor can live for more than 20 years.

"Redrock" is the name of Green's red-tailed boa constrictor. This type of snake is native to tropical regions of North, Central, and South America. They can grow in length from 3 to 13 feet (1 to 4 meters) and normally weigh up to 60 pounds (27 kg). They can bite, but they are not normally a threat to humans. Boa constrictors are most famous for constricting (or squeezing) their prey before eating it. This action kills the prey by cutting off the animal's blood flow. Redrock, who is about 5 feet (1.5 m) long, uses this signal to notify Green of an **impending** seizure.

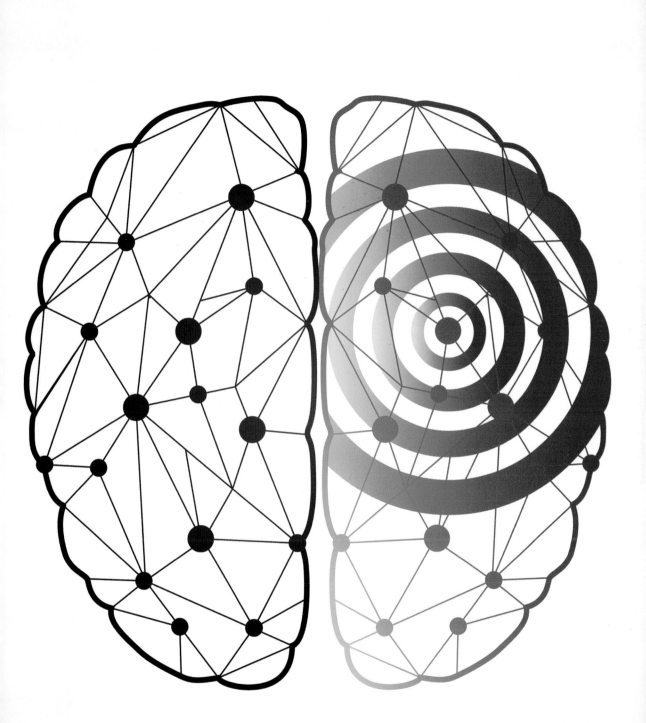

Seizures are caused by abnormal brain cell activity.

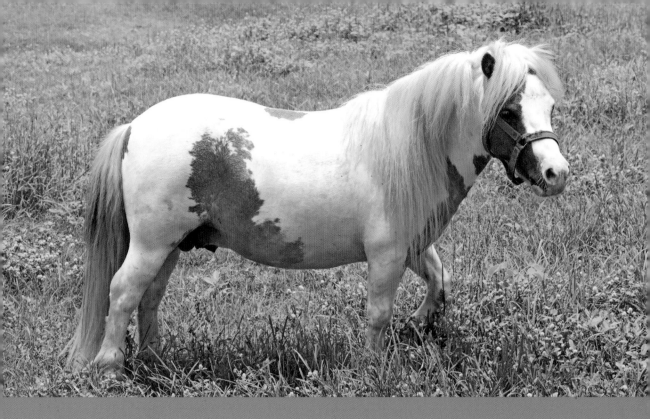

The Americans with Disabilities Act recognizes miniature horses as service animals.

Snakes are extremely sensitive. They "hear" by feeling vibrations through their lower jaw. In the wild, they can sense minute "ripples" in the sand caused by approaching prey. Green believes that when Redrock is wrapped around his neck, it senses the changes in his body right before a seizure is about to occur. When Redrock feels the change, it gives Green a small "hug." He then knows to take his seizure medication or to remove himself from a stressful situation. He has trained Redrock to go into a carrier bag right after notifying him of a likely seizure.

Green has more seizures at nighttime, because Redrock does not sleep with him.

Unfortunately, Redrock is not considered a service animal and is sometimes not allowed to be with Green in public places. As of 2011, the Americans with Disabilities Act only recognizes dogs and miniature horses as service animals. This means that business owners can ban Redrock. Though it would be alarming to see a man in a restaurant with a boa constrictor draped around his neck, Green depends on Redrock. They cooperate with each other so that Redrock can give life-saving signals and Green can take action.

Cooperation in the Workplace

Having a successful career starts with being cooperative. Everyone, and especially the people you work with, will appreciate your cooperation. Cooperating with others will make you happier because you can make decisions you all agree with, whether it's what project to work on or even what to have for lunch! Further, by listening and being patient, your boss can do their best to help you if you have a question. Understanding your coworkers helps you have better friendships in the workplace, and you can easily solve disagreements you may have.

Cooperation Afloat Readiness and Training

Cooperation between countries is critical to the security and safety of the world. Countries that work together through meetings, discussions, and training develop strong, cooperative relationships. These relationships build a sense of responsibility and **kinship** to each other, which helps to prevent future conflict.

Since 1995, the United States Navy has been organizing **maritime** training sessions with partner navies around the world. Cooperation Afloat Readiness and Training (CARAT) is a series of annual naval exercises between the United States and Bangladesh, Brunei, Cambodia, Indonesia, Malaysia, the Philippines, Singapore, Thailand, and Timor-Leste. It is designed

This photo shows CARAT training between the US and Thailand in 2013.

to improve security skills at sea and cooperation among participating countries. CARAT training makes sure the United States and these Asian countries can complete tasks together.

The US Navy sails missile destroyers, combat ships, landing dock ships, and diving and **salvage** ships to these countries' waters in order to train sailors on the most up-to-date military equipment. The training lasts multiple days and is held at sea and on land. It covers multiple warfare areas: surface, air, submarine, and information. Sea training activities can include small-boat

Living in close quarters on a ship requires a lot of cooperation.

operations, diving and salvage exercises, helicopter flight operations, and communication exercises. Shore training activities can include search and seizure operations, explosive **ordnance** disposal, disaster response, **humanitarian** assistance, and medical training. Many naval ships and planes are used during the exercises.

The training also includes community service opportunities that both navies can participate in, which helps them get to know and help the local population.

Rear Admiral Don Gabrielson of the US Navy talked about the cooperative training with the Royal Thai Navy. He said, "Our engagement through CARAT provides the US and Thailand an opportunity to strengthen our alliance and maritime partnership in very meaningful ways." Combined military band concerts also develop a spirit of friendship and are a source of entertainment for the community.

It is important that our military engages with other countries in cooperative training, especially if US relationships with other countries waver. Sometimes poor relationships with one of the partner countries prevent an annual CARAT event from occurring. But through diplomatic discussions, the training returns. Through CARAT activities, the participating sailors and their commanders develop cultural and personal connections with each other. Gabrielson says these connections can "deepen relationships at all levels and create bonds of trust that span generations within our forces."

Paris Climate Accord

Have you ever tried to get a bunch of your friends to agree to something? Even if it is very important, it is hard to get people with differing opinions to develop a similar viewpoint about an issue. Only then can the group make a decision that satisfies everyone. In 2015, the countries of the world worked hard and cooperated with each other to develop a plan to protect the planet.

The Paris Climate Accord is an agreement that establishes a plan to limit the **emission** of greenhouse gases in order to limit **climate change**. On December 12, 2015, representatives from 196 countries and groups approved the agreement at the

United Nations Climate Change Conference in Paris, France. Representatives from 175 countries officially signed the agreement on April 22, 2016. The creation of the accord shows the resolve of the cooperating nations to protect the planet.

One result of climate change is global warming. Global warming refers to the rising temperatures around the world that scientists have observed in the past century. Since the 1950s, temperatures have risen more quickly, spurring the idea that human activities have led to an increase in greenhouse gases. Greenhouse gases act like a large blanket wrapped around the planet, trapping heat instead of letting it escape into space. Normal levels of greenhouse gases (including water vapor, ozone, methane, nitrous oxide, and carbon dioxide) in our atmosphere maintain a livable environment for people and animals on Earth. But a rise in carbon dioxide over the last few decades has caused higher global temperatures. This rise in temperature cannot be explained by natural weather alone.

Human activities that have increased carbon dioxide in the atmosphere include the use of automobiles, coal burning for energy, and the burning and clearing of forested land for raising animals. The effects of global warming are already noticeable in some areas of the world. These areas are seeing changing rainfall, extreme weather events, rising sea levels, the spreading of deserts, and the extinction of animal species. Warming in the Arctic has caused huge glaciers made of ice and snow to melt into the oceans, forcing animals and humans to abandon their homes.

Melting sea ice can cause environmental issues.

Dairy production adds to the effects of global warming.

According to the Paris Climate Accord, each country determines how it should limit global warming. **Developing countries** are given more freedom in **mitigating** climate change as they work to advance their society. Although the United States withdrew from the accord, many Americans are still committed to protecting the environment. These citizens and the other countries that signed the accord exhibit cooperation and a determination to do what is best for the planet.

What Have You Learned About Cooperation?

Being cooperative shows that you are ready and willing to help others when needed. You are putting the good of the group in front of your own needs in order to solve a problem. The benefits of being cooperative include building friendships, strengthening relationships, helping each other, and making the world a better place. We all benefit when we cooperate with each other. Who do you cooperate with? Think about how your life has been made better through cooperation.

Think About It

How Can You Become More Cooperative?

Cooperating with others involves listening, understanding, and being patient. This sounds easy, but it is hard work. Have you ever interrupted someone when they were speaking? See how easy it is to not be cooperative? To be more cooperative, you need to understand the thoughts and feelings of others so that you can work together to come up with a solution that makes everyone happy. Listen to others and you will be more cooperative.

For More Information

Further Reading

Animals and Your Health: The Power of Pets to Heal Our Pain, Help Us Cope, and Improve Our Well-Being. New York: TIME, 2016.

Lusted, Marcia Amidon. *The International Space Station.* Farmington Hills, MI: Lucent Books, 2006.

Simon, Seymour. *Global Warming.* New York: HarperCollins, 2010.

Webb, Brandon. *The Making of a Navy SEAL: My Story of Surviving the Toughest Challenge and Training the Best.* New York: St. Martin's Press, 2015.

Websites

History—Treaty of Versailles
https://www.history.com/topics/world-war-i/treaty-of-versailles
Read more about the Treaty of Versailles and World War I.

Kids' Health—Epilepsy: Having "Fits"
www.cyh.com/HealthTopics/HealthTopicDetailsKids.aspx?p=335&np=285&id=1710
This site helps kids better understand epilepsy.

NASA—Space Station Research & Technology: Space Station for Students
https://www.nasa.gov/mission_pages/station/research/ops/research_student.html
Follow the links at this site to visit the participating space agencies' student websites.

GLOSSARY

adverse (ad-VURS) bad

agencies (AY-juhn-seez) government departments that are responsible for particular activities or operations

Allied forces (AL-ide FORS-iz) a group of over 30 countries that had an agreement during World War I, including the United Kingdom, France, the United States, and Italy

armistice (AHR-mih-stis) an agreement to stop fighting a war, also called a truce

assassination (uh-SAS-uh-nay-shun) killing a famous or important person, usually for political reasons

Central Powers (SEN-truhl POU-erz) a group of countries that had an agreement during World War I, including Germany, Austria-Hungary, Bulgaria, and the Ottoman Empire

climate change (KLYE-mit CHAYNJ) a change in normal weather patterns over a long period of time

consciousness (KON-shuhs-nis) the normal state of being awake and able to understand what is happening around you

developing countries (dih-VEL-uhp-ing KUHN-treez) countries where most people are poor and there is not much industry

diplomatic (dip-luh-MAT-ik) relating to the work of maintaining good relations between the governments of different countries

emission (ih-MISH-uhn) the act of producing or sending out something (such as energy or gas) from a source

epilepsy (EP-uh-lep-see) a disorder of the nervous system that can cause people to suddenly become unconscious and to have violent, uncontrolled movements of the body

humanitarian (hyoo-man-ih-TER-ee-uhn) having to do with helping people and improving their lives

impending (im-PEN-ding) likely to happen soon

kinship (KIN-ship) a feeling of being close or connected to other people

maritime (MAR-ih-time) having to do with the sea, ships, or navigation

mitigating (MIT-ih-gayt-ing) making something less severe or harmful

negotiate (nih-GOH-shee-ayt) to discuss something formally in order to make an agreement

neurons (NOO-ronz) cells that carry messages between the brain and other parts of the body

neutron stars (NU-tron STAHRZ) glowing leftovers of a star that exploded

ordnance (ORD-nuns) military weapons

participating (pahr-TIS-uh-pate-ing) joining with others in an activity or event

physics (FIZ-iks) the study of movement, force, light, heat, sound, and electricity

reparations (rep-uh-RAY-shuhnz) payments of money or materials made by a country or group that loses a war because of the damage it has caused

salvage (SAL-vij) property rescued from a shipwreck or other disaster

surge (SURJ) a sudden increase in amount or speed

treaties (TREE-teez) official agreements made between two or more countries or groups

INDEX